COPY   56 x

J
398.2   Gackenbach, Dick.
G   Arabella and Mr. Crack : an old Eng-
           lish tale / retold by Dick Gackenbach.
           New York : Macmillan, c1982.
               [32] p. : ill. ; 17 x 18 cm.   k-2

               SUMMARY: Mr. Crack's new housekeeper
           quickly learns to use his idiosyncratic
           vocabulary.
               ISBN 0-02-735770-8 : 5.00

               1.Folklore--England. 2.Vocabulary--Fic-
           tion.

                                    65769   F83
                                            81-15670
                                            MARC AC

Arabella and Mr. Crack

AN OLD ENGLISH TALE RETOLD BY

Dick Gackenbach

MACMILLAN PUBLISHING CO., INC. / NEW YORK

Macmillan Publishing Co., Inc.
866 Third Avenue, New York, N.Y. 10022
Collier Macmillan Canada, Ltd.
Printed in the United States of America

10   9   8   7   6   5   4   3   2   1

Library of Congress Cataloging in Publication Data
Gackenbach, Dick.
Arabella and Mr. Crack.
Summary: Mr. Crack's new housekeeper quickly
learns to use his idiosyncratic vocabulary.
[1. Folklore—England. 2. Vocabulary—Fiction]
I. Title.
PZ8.1.G13Ar   1982   398.2'0941   [E]   81-15670
ISBN 0-02-735770-8   AACR2

For Jim Steiger

$\mathcal{A}$rabella Marbles took a job, working for Mr. Crack.

"If you live here and clean and cook for me," Mr. Crack told Arabella, "there are some things you have to learn."

"What are they?" asked Arabella.

"I have special names for certain things," said Mr. Crack. "I will teach you what they are, and you must always use them when you speak to me."

"Whatever you please," agreed Arabella.

"What name do you have for this?" asked Mr. Crack, pointing to his bed.

"Why, that is a bed," said Arabella.

"It is not a bed here," said Mr. Crack. "From now on, you must call it a bubbleloo."

"As you wish," said Arabella.

"And what are these?" questioned Mr. Crack, holding onto his pants.

"Trousers, of course, sir!" answered Arabella.

"No, no!" said Mr. Crack. "They are my salty toasters."

"If you say so," said Arabella.

"And these?" asked Mr. Crack, holding up his leg to show his boot. "What name do you have for these?"

"My goodness," replied Arabella, "they are only boots."

"Not at all," insisted Mr. Crack. "They are my whomper whackers."

"I will remember that," said Arabella.

"Now," said Mr. Crack, pointing to his dog. "What would you call her?"

"A good-for-nothing old hound dog, to be sure," said Arabella.

"Nothing of the kind," said Mr. Crack. "She is a fur-toed boozer dozer."

"That's some name for a dog," muttered Arabella.

"And this?" said Mr. Crack, showing Arabella the open fire. "What is this?"

"It's a roaring fire," she replied.

"Wrong again," cried Mr. Crack. "It's a hot sizzlelorum, silly girl."

"Fancy that," said Arabella.

Mr. Crack held up a bucket. "What do you think this is?" he wanted to know.

"You could call it a pail," suggested Arabella.

"Not I," said Mr. Crack. "I call it a ducket-racket, and so must you."

"If you insist," said Arabella with a sigh.

"Now tell me what it holds," said Mr. Crack, as he poured water from the bucket.

"What it holds is wet," shouted Arabella. "And you're getting it all over the floor!"

"What I'm pouring on the floor is called pondoleeky,"explained Mr. Crack.

"Whatever you call it, it's still wet," mumbled Arabella.

Mr. Crack grabbed Arabella by her hand

and took her outside.

There, he proudly pointed at his house. "Last, but not least," he said, "that is my high shackadorum."

"You could have fooled me," said Arabella. "I thought it was a house."

"I am very fussy about my special names," Mr. Crack told Arabella. "So, be sure you remember everything I've taught you."

"I'll do my best, sir!" Arabella promised. But, to herself, Arabella wondered what she had gotten herself into.

On that very night, Arabella woke Mr. Crack
by yelling and banging on his bedroom door.

"What is the matter, girl?" cried the
startled Mr. Crack.

Arabella answered
as fast as she
was able.

"Hurry," she shouted. "Get out of your bubbleloo. Pull on your salty toasters and jump into your whomper whackers quickly.

"The fur-toed boozer dozer has a spark of hot sizzlelorum on her tail.

Unless you toss a ducket-racket of
pondoleeky on her,

your high shackadorum will catch on hot
sizzlelorum. That's all!

And get yourself a new housekeeper, I quit!"